Lil' Bratz™
Beauty Sleepover Bash!

www.bratzpack.com

Used under license by Penguin Young Readers Group. Published in 2005 by Grosset & Dunlap, a division of Penguin Young Readers Group, 345 Hudson Street, New York, New York 10014. GROSSET & DUNLAP is a trademark of Penguin Group (USA) Inc. Printed in the U.S.A.

Library of Congress Cataloging-in-Publication Data

Beauty sleepover bash!
p. cm.
"Lil' Bratz."
Summary: When it looks like Nazalia's birthday party will have to be cancelled, her friends come up with a plan to surprise her.
ISBN 0-448-43730-9 (pbk.)
[1. Parties—Fiction. 2. Sleepovers—Fiction. 3. Friendship—Fiction.]
PZ7.B380585 2005
[E]—dc22

2004009670

ISBN 0-448-43730-9 10 9 8 7 6 5 4 3 2 1

Li'l Bratz™
Beauty Sleepover Bash!
GROSSET & DUNLAP • NEW YORK

Nazalia sat in her bedroom, thinking. Her birthday was in less than three weeks, and she wanted to have a party. But what kind?

A pool party? Nazalia shook her head. *Nah.*

A beach party? Nazalia imagined her friends hanging out at the beach. *That's fun, but I want to do something just with my best buds,* she thought. *A cool, fun party just for me and my best friends.*

Suddenly, Nazalia had an amazing idea.

A beauty sleepover! she thought. *Perfect!*

Nazalia whipped out colored glitter pens and made three awesome, sparkly invitations. She couldn't wait to give them to her best friends Ailani, Zada, and Talia tomorrow at school.

Come to my
Beauty Sleepover Birthday Bash!

When: On my birthday (of course!)

Where: Nazalia's house

Time: 6:00 p.m.

Bring: Your pj's, your fave music, make-up, movies, and YOURSELF!

The next morning, Nazalia met Talia at her locker.

"Hey, I've got something for you," Nazalia told her. She pulled out an invitation.

Talia smiled. "A sleepover? Cool! I'm totally there!"

Then Talia looked at the invitation and frowned.

"Bummer! My championship track meet is the same night!" she said. "The game is out of town. There's no way the team bus will be back in time!"

Nazalia was disappointed.

"Oh, no!" she said. "How will we have a sleepover without you?"

"Well, I can come after my track meet, but it will be really late," Talia said.

"Better late than never!" Nazalia said with a smile.

Nazalia gave Ailani her invitation at lunch. Right away, Ailani started thinking of all the fun stuff they would do. "We'll give one another makeovers and manicures and pedicures. And crazy cool do's—of course!"

Nazalia laughed. Ailani's excitement made her feel a lot better.

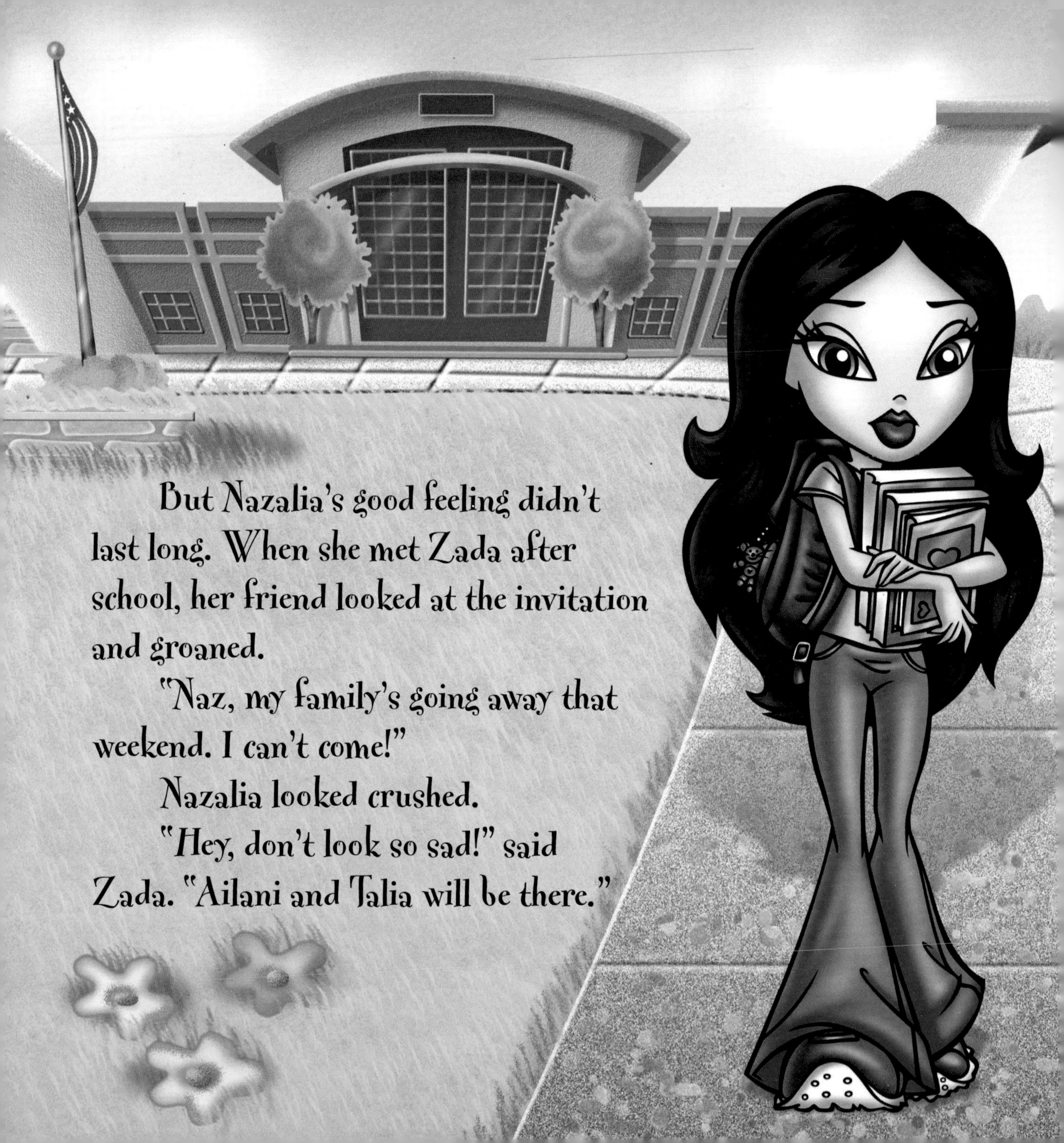

But Nazalia's good feeling didn't last long. When she met Zada after school, her friend looked at the invitation and groaned.

"Naz, my family's going away that weekend. I can't come!"

Nazalia looked crushed.

"Hey, don't look so sad!" said Zada. "Ailani and Talia will be there."

Nazalia shook her head. "Talia's going to be really late because of her big track meet. And I can't have a celebration without all of my best friends there."

"Can we do it another night?" Zada asked.

"I have rehearsals for the class play every other weekend night," Nazalia explained glumly. "I guess I'll have to put off having a sleepover until the play is over."

That night, Zada tried to work on her history report, but she couldn't stop thinking about how bummed Nazalia had been. Zada got on her cell phone and dialed Ailani.

"Ali, we've just *got* to do something fabulous for Naz's birthday!" Zada said.

"I know!" said Ailani. "This definitely calls for an emergency meeting! Pita Palace. Saturday at noon. Will you call Talia and let her know?"

"Absolutely," Zada said. "It's a plan!"

That Saturday, the girls met at the Pita Palace.

"I've got an idea," said Talia. "Since Nazalia's busy with rehearsals, why don't we talk to Mr. Clarkson? *He's* directing the play. I'm sure he'll let Nazalia miss just one rehearsal."

"Awesome idea!" Ailani said. "And let's make Nazalia's sleepover a surprise!"

"I love it!" Zada said. "Let's have the party next Friday, the weekend *before* her birthday? She'll be totally shocked!"

"Done!" Talia said. "We'd better split up if we're going to have time to shop for everything we'll need."

Ailani headed to the bath and body store. She loaded up on hot new make-up samples, cool nail colors, funky hair bobbles, and sweet-smelling lotions and face masks.

Zada was appointed party designer, so she headed to the party store for some funky decorating supplies.

"Balloons? Check.

"Streamers? All right!

"Confetti? Excellent!"

She looked at her list. Something was missing.

"Paints!" Zada selected all of Nazalia's favorite colors. "Time for me to get crafty!"

Talia had to wait until Monday to do her part. She got to school early to talk to Mr. Clarkson about their birthday surprise for Nazalia.

Mr. Clarkson listened thoughtfully. When Talia was done, she held her breath. He looked so serious! Was he going to say no?

But then he smiled.

Fantastic!

3/4 x 12=

That week, Ailani, Zada, and Talia were so excited they could hardly keep their secret. One day, they were so giddy that even Nazalia started to pick up on their vibe.

"What's going on with you guys?" she asked. "You're so silly today!"

"Oh, I guess we're just in a good mood because it's so sunny outside," Ailani said breezily. Zada nodded quickly in agreement.

On Friday, Nazalia and Ailani met at their lockers after school.

"Guess what?" Nazalia said. "I have awesome news! Mr. Clarkson just told me I've been working so hard at rehearsals that I deserve the night off. Can you believe it?"

Ailani put on her best surprised face.

"No way!" she replied. "That's incredible! I didn't know Mr. Clarkson believed in giving students a break. Let's get out of here before he sees you and changes his mind!"

When they reached Ailani's house, Nazalia was still super-psyched about her night off.

"I haven't had a Friday off in forever," she chattered as Ailani unlocked the door. "I mean, really—"

"SURPRISE!"

Nazalia gasped.

Ailani laughed. "Did you think we were actually going to let you cancel your birthday party?"

"You guys totally rock!" Nazalia said as she gave her friends a huge hug.

Then it was time to party! First, the girls changed into their pj's. Then they ate pizza, watched a fabulous film starring their fave actress, and had a talent contest.

Then it was time to honor the birthday diva with a beauty makeover. The girls did Nazalia's hair in a funky do and painted her fingers and toes a sparkly purple—her favorite color!

"We should all have makeovers, not just me," Nazalia said when they were done.

So the girls paired up and worked together until each one had a kickin' makeover of her own!

Soon it was time for some beauty sleep. Nazalia was so tired that she could hardly stay awake, but she couldn't drift off into dreamland without thanking her friends.

"Thanks, guys," she said softly. "You're the best friends a girl can have. Good night!"